HUGS-A-LOTL CAN'T SHOW THE LOVE

by C.W. Estes
illustrated by Irene Saluzzi

PICTURE WINDOW BOOKS
a capstone imprint

Published by Picture Window Books, an imprint of Capstone
1710 Roe Crest Drive, North Mankato, Minnesota 56003
capstonepub.com

Copyright © 2025 by Capstone. All rights reserved. No part of this publication may be reproduced in whole or in part, or stored in a retrieval system, or transmitted in any form or by any means, electronic, mechanical, photocopying, recording, or otherwise, without written permission of the publisher.

Library of Congress Cataloging-in-Publication Data
Names: Estes, C. W., author. | Saluzzi, Irene, illustrator.
Title: Hugs-a-lotl can't show the love / by C. W. Estes ; illustrated by Irene Saluzzi. Other titles: Hugs-a-lotl can not show the love
Description: North Mankato, Minnesota : Picture Window Books, 2025. | Series: Axolotls! | Audience: Ages 5–8. | Audience: Grades K–1. | Summary: Hugs-a-Lotl is an axolotl who loves to hug his friends in Sandy Shorts, but when his arms fall off, he needs to find a substitute who will hug for him while the arms grow back. Includes glossary, facts about axolotls, and discussion questions.
Identifiers: LCCN 2024020623 (print) | LCCN 2024020624 (ebook) | ISBN 9780756584221 (hardcover) | ISBN 9780756584184 (paperback) | ISBN 9780756584191 (pdf) | ISBN 9780756584252 (kindle edition) | ISBN 9780756584207 (epub)
Subjects: LCSH: Axolotls—Juvenile fiction. | Hugging—Juvenile fiction. | Friendship—Juvenile fiction. | Regeneration (Biology)—Juvenile fiction. | CYAC: Axolotls—Fiction. | Amphibians—Fiction. | Hugging—Fiction | Friendship—Fiction. | Regeneration (Biology)—Fiction. | LCGFT: Picture books.
Classification: LCC PZ7.1.E8523 Hu 2025 (print) | LCC PZ7.1.E8523 (ebook) | DDC 813.6 [E]—dc23/eng/20240701
LC record available at https://lccn.loc.gov/2024020623
LC ebook record available at https://lccn.loc.gov/2024020624

Designed by Dina Her

Any additional websites and resources referenced in this book are not maintained, authorized, or sponsored by Capstone. All product and company names are trademarks™ or registered® trademarks of their respective holders.

TABLE OF CONTENTS

CHAPTER 1
HUG, HUG ME DO.................... 7

CHAPTER 2
MEGA-AWESOME HUG-ATHON 13

CHAPTER 3
STOP IN THE NAME OF HUG 22

Deep underwater lies the bubbly town of Sandy Shorts. Every animal is a friend here. But no animal is friendlier than the axolotls!

They always smile. They love what they love. And they each name themselves after their own favorite thing.

CHAPTER 1

HUG, HUG ME DO

Hugs-a-Lotl loves to hug. He is very good at it. The animals of Sandy Shorts line up every morning to get a hug from him!

But Mr. Stoppit the lionfish is always too busy for hugs. He has an important job. He directs traffic.

"Can I hug you today, Mr. Stoppit?" asks Hugs-a-Lotl.

"Sorry, Hugs. I'm making sure these cars get to where they need to go," replies Mr. Stoppit.

Then the lionfish waves his gloved fins. He blows his whistle. *TWEEE!*

After Hugs-a-Lotl finishes his morning hugs, he floats to the playground. He likes to jump rope. It makes his arms strong. And that makes his hugs even more huggy.

Today he jumps fast. **Super fast.
Too fast!**

Hugs-a-Lotl spins the rope so fast, his arms fly off his body. *POP!*

Don't worry. His arms will grow back. But until they do, there will not be any hugging.

CHAPTER 2

MEGA-AWESOME HUG-ATHON

Hugs-a-Lotl's friends want to help. They have all lost an arm or a leg before.

"But you've never lost two at the same time!" cries Hugs.

At school, Snacks-a-Lotl helps Hugs eat pizza.

Draws-a-Lotl helps Hugs paint a picture.

And Knows-a-Lotl raises her hand for Hugs in class. She raises it even when he doesn't know the answer!

Hugs-a-Lotl likes all the help.

But one question keeps bugging him.

Who will hug for me? he wonders.

The question makes it hard for Hugs to sleep that night. He tosses and turns.

Then he rolls out of bed with no arms to stop him. Oh no! *BONK!*

The next day, Hugs-a-Lotl wakes up tired. But he has a plan.

"There will be a mega-awesome hug-athon in five minutes!" he shouts in the middle of town.

Everyone cheers! Well, everyone except Mr. Stoppit. He is busy keeping all of the cars safe.

Everyone in town gathers for the mega-awesome hug-athon.

Hugs-a-Lotl has to find someone to hug for him while his arms grow back. He wants to find the best hugger in Sandy Shorts.

"It's okay if you don't want to, but can I please get a hug from you all?" asks Hugs-a-Lotl.

The animals agree. They each give the axolotl a test hug.

The hugs are all nice. But none of them are quite right.

Too pointy. 	Too rough. 	Too hard. 
Too slimy. 	Too squishy. 	Too long. 
Too short. 	Too clammy. 	Too sharky. 
Too slappy. 	Too crabby. 	Too many! 

CHAPTER 3

STOP IN THE NAME OF HUG

On his way home, Hugs-a-Lotl feels very sad. He sees Mr. Stoppit sitting on a bench.

"Hi, Mr. Stoppit," says Hugs. "Why aren't you directing traffic?"

"There are no cars to direct," replies the lionfish. "Everyone was at your mega-awesome hug-athon."

"Wait. You didn't go?" says Hugs. "That means you haven't hugged me yet!"

Hugs-a-Lotl asks, "Can you hug me today, Mr. Stoppit?"

The lionfish nods. He gives the axolotl a test hug.

It isn't like the others. It isn't too long, too short, or too slappy.

Mr. Stoppit's hug is warm, but not hot. It is firm, but not hard. And it lasts for three and a half seconds. The perfect amount of time.

Hugs has found his hug double! Yahoo!

Things are normal again in Sandy Shorts. Mr. Stoppit fills in for Hugs-a-Lotl every morning. His long fins help him give more hugs. He even does Double Hug Tuesday!

Mr. Stoppit is busy hugging.
So Hugs-a-Lotl directs traffic for him.
Hugs isn't very good at it. But he
has fun. And the gloves keep his baby
hands warm while they grow back.

THE REAL-LIFE CRITTERS

AXOLOTL FACTS

★ Wild axolotls are found in just one place. They live in two freshwater lakes near Mexico City, Mexico.

★ Real axolotls don't lose arms jumping rope. But another animal might bite off an axolotl's leg or tail. Axolotls can regrow the missing body part. It takes at least four weeks.

★ Axolotls are amphibians. Most amphibians live in water when they're young and go on land when they're adults. Not axolotls! They stay underwater their whole lives.

★ Feathery gills around an axolotl's face let it breathe underwater.

★ Wild axolotls are usually dark brown or gray. Pet axolotls can be many colors. They can be pink, yellow, white, purple, and dark green.

LIONFISH FACTS

★ You wouldn't find a lionfish and axolotl together in the wild. Lionfish live in salt water. They are from the Indian and Pacific Oceans. But they have spread to many other oceans.

★ Real lionfish wouldn't be up during the day directing traffic. They swim and hunt for food at night.

★ Lionfish would be terrible huggers in real life. The fins on their backs have spines with venom! It can harm people and animals.

GLOSSARY

athon (UH-thon)—an event that involves a lot of something; a hug-athon has a lot of hugging

axolotl (AK-suh-lot-uhl)—an amphibian with four legs and webbed feet, a long tail, and gills around its face; axolotls spend their whole lives in water

direct (dih-REKT)—to show when and where to go

double (DUH-buhl)—someone or something that is like another person or thing and can take their place

float (FLOHT)—to move gently through water

normal (NOR-muhl)—something that is usual and that someone is used to

squishy (SKWISH-ee)—soft and easy to press down

test (TEST)—used for finding out how well something works or acts

traffic (TRAF-ik)—the movement of cars, buses, trucks, and other vehicles along a road

DIVE DEEPER

1. How did Hugs-a-Lotl feel after his arms popped off? What makes you think that?

2. In what ways did the animals in Sandy Shorts help Hugs throughout this story? Make a list.

3. Why did Hugs have trouble sleeping? What do you do when you can't fall asleep?

4. The characters in this book are based on real animals. But the story is fiction. Flip back and point to at least three parts of the story that help you know it is fiction.

5. Hugs-a-Lotl loves to give hugs. What is your favorite thing to do?

ABOUT THE AUTHOR

C.W. Estes lives with his wife, two sons, one dog, and three chickens outside of Los Angeles, California. He loves reading, writing, and hearing his stories read out loud by young readers. He truly hopes that you enjoy these tales and wishes you all the best in your reading journey!

ABOUT THE ILLUSTRATOR

Irene Saluzzi grew up near the sea in Ancona, Italy, and graduated with a degree in architecture before studying entertainment design. Now, she lives in Florence and works as a freelance illustrator. She loves listening to all types of music, as well as reading novels and picture books. She looks at the world with the eyes of a child and aims to spread joy through her drawings.